WHAT WOULD YOU iMAGiNE?

nǐ   huì   xiǎng   dào   shén   me
你 会 想 到 什 么?

Text and Art by **Justin Tsin**

yuán zhù hé měi gōng qín zhèng xián
原 著 和 美 工: 覃 正 贤

Altea

To my grandparents and all the people I love.

© This edition:
2008, Santillana USA Publishing Company, Inc.
2105 NW 86th Avenue
Miami, FL 33122
www.santillanausa.com

Text and Art © 2008 Justin Tsin
3EArtist@gmail.com

Managing Editor: Isabel C. Mendoza
Design: Silvana Izquierdo
Photography: Dr. Yee Wan

English Version Reviewers: Dr. Yee Wan and Ruthie Hutchings
Copyediting of English Text: Isabel C. Mendoza and Simone T. Ribke
Chinese Translation: Dr. Yee Wan and Xiao Yun Deng
Chinese Version Reviewers: Helen Wong, Dr. Ji-Mei Chang, Dr. Christy Lau, and Zhi Juan Dai

Altea is part of the Santillana Group, with offices in the following countries:

ARGENTINA, BOLIVIA, CHILE, COLOMBIA, COSTA RICA, DOMINICAN REPUBLIC,
ECUADOR, EL SALVADOR, GUATEMALA, MEXICO, PANAMA, PARAGUAY, PERU, PUERTO
RICO, SPAIN, UNITED STATES, URUGUAY, AND VENEZUELA.

What Would You Imagine?
ISBN 10: 1-60396-039-2
ISBN 13: 978-1-60396-039-7

Published in the United States of America
Printed by HCI Printing & Publishing, Inc.

12 11 10 09 08   1 2 3 4 5 6 7

If you had **3** peacocks, what would you imagine?

rú guǒ nǐ yǒu sān zhī kǒng què
如 果 你 有 三 只 孔 雀,
nǐ huì xiǎng dào shén me
你 会 想 到 什 么?

I would imagine three fancy feather fans.

wǒ huì xiǎng dào sān bǎ huá lì de
我 会 想 到 三 把 华 丽 的
yǔ máo shàn zi
羽 毛 扇 子。

If you had **6** caterpillars, what would you imagine?

rú guǒ nǐ yǒu liù tiáo xiǎo máo mao chóng
如果你有六条小毛毛虫，
nǐ huì xiǎng dào shén me
你会想到什么？

I would imagine tasty treats for my parrots.

wǒ huì xiǎng dào wǒ de yīng wǔ de
我 会 想 到 我 的 鹦 鹉 的
měi wèi diǎn xin
美 味 点 心 。

If you had **9** dragons, what would you imagine?

rú guǒ nǐ yǒu jiǔ tiáo lóng
如 果 你 有 九 条 龙 ,
nǐ huì xiǎng dào shén me
你 会 想 到 什 么 ?

I would imagine nine shimmering dragon boats.

wǒ huì xiǎng dào jiǔ tiáo jīn guāng
我 会 想 到 九 条 金 光
shǎn shǎn de lóng chuán
闪 闪 的 龙 船 。

If you had **12** crabs, what would you imagine?

rú guǒ nǐ yǒu shí èr zhī páng xiè
如 果 你 有 十 二 只 螃 蟹，
nǐ huì xiǎng dào shén me
你 会 想 到 什 么？

I would imagine a jolly marching contest.

wǒ huì xiǎng dào yì chǎng hǎo wán de
我 会 想 到 一 场 好 玩 的
zǒu lù cāo bǐ sài
走 路 操 比 赛。

If you had **15** penguins, what would you imagine?

rú guǒ nǐ yǒu shí wǔ zhī qǐ é
如 果 你 有 十 五 只 企 鹅,
nǐ huì xiǎng dào shén me
你 会 想 到 什 么?

I would imagine an amusing board game.

wǒ huì xiǎng dào yí pán yǒu qù de qí
我 会 想 到 一 盘 有 趣 的 棋 。

If you had **18** bats, what would you imagine?

rú guǒ nǐ yǒu shí bā zhī biān fú
如 果 你 有 十 八 只 蝙 蝠，
nǐ huì xiǎng dào shén me
你 会 想 到 什 么？

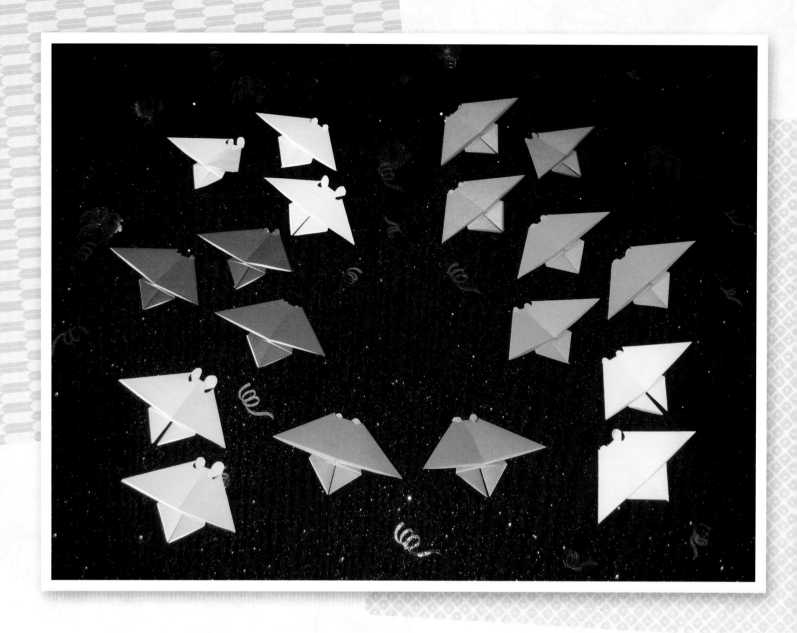

I would imagine a spectacular fluttering air show.

wǒ huì xiǎng dào yì chǎng zhuàng guān
我 会 想 到 一 场 壮 观
de kōng zhōng fēi xíng biǎo yǎn
的 空 中 飞 行 表 演。

If you had **21** seals, what would you imagine?

rú guǒ nǐ yǒu èr shí yī zhī hǎi bào
如 果 你 有 二 十 一 只 海 豹 ，
nǐ huì xiǎng dào shén me
你 会 想 到 什 么 ？

I would imagine an astounding acrobatic show.

wǒ huì xiǎng dào yì chǎng jīng cǎi de
我 会 想 到 一 场 精彩的
zá jì biǎo yǎn
杂技表演。

If you had **24** ladybugs, what would you imagine?

rú guǒ nǐ yǒu èr shí sì zhī xiǎo piáo chóng
如 果 你 有 二 十 四 只 小 瓢 虫 ，
nǐ huì xiǎng dào shén me
你 会 想 到 什 么 ？

I would imagine an enormous ferris wheel ride.

wǒ huì xiǎng dào yì gè jù dà de
我 会 想 到 一 个 巨 大 的
mó tiān lún
摩 天 轮 。

If you had **27** birds, what would you imagine?

rú guǒ nǐ yǒu èr shí qī zhī niǎo
如 果 你 有 二 十 七 只 鸟，
nǐ huì xiǎng dào shén me
你 会 想 到 什 么?

I would imagine a delightful choir.

wǒ huì xiǎng dào yì zhī huān lè de
我 会 想 到 一 支 欢 乐 的
hé chàng tuán
合 唱 团 。

If you had **30** frogs, what would you imagine?

rú guǒ nǐ yǒu sān shí zhī qīng wā
如 果 你 有 三 十 只 青 蛙,
nǐ huì xiǎng dào shén me
你 会 想 到 什 么?

I would imagine an exciting long-jump match.

wǒ huì xiǎng dào yì chǎng jī liè de
我 会 想 到 一 场 激烈 的
tiào yuǎn bǐ sài
跳 远 比 赛 。

If you had **99** chickens, what would you imagine?

rú guǒ nǐ yǒu jiǔ shí jiǔ zhī mǔ jī
如 果 你 有 九 十 九 只 母 鸡，
nǐ huì xiǎng dào shén me
你 会 想 到 什 么？

I would imagine a year's supply of colorful eggs.

wǒ huì xiǎng dào zài yì nián lǐ
我 会 想 到 在 一 年 里
chī yě chī bù wán de cǎi dàn
吃 也 吃 不 完 的 彩 蛋。

If you had 3 peacocks, 6 caterpillars, 9 dragons, 12 crabs, 15 penguins, 18 bats, 21 seals, 24 ladybugs, 27 birds, 30 frogs, and 99 chickens, what would YOU imagine?

rú guǒ nǐ yǒu sān zhī kǒng què　　liù tiáo
如果你有三只孔雀、六条

xiǎo máo mao chóng　jiǔ tiáo lóng　shí èr
小毛毛虫、九条龙、十二

zhī páng xiè　shí wǔ zhī qǐ é　shí bā
只螃蟹、十五只企鹅、十八

zhī biān fú　èr shí yī zhī hǎi bào　èr
只蝙蝠、二十一只海豹、二

shí sì zhī xiǎo piáo chóng　èr shí qī zhī
十四只小瓢虫、二十七只

niǎo　sān shí zhī qīng wā hé jiǔ shí jiǔ zhī
鸟、三十只青蛙和九十九只

mǔ jī　nǐ huì xiǎng dào shén me
母鸡，你会想到什么？

My name is Justin Tsin. I was born on October 20, 1999 in San Jose, California, U.S.A. I live with my mom and dad in San Jose. In addition to going to my regular school, I go to a Chinese after-school program to learn Mandarin. I speak English, Mandarin, and Cantonese.

I have a large extended family. Some of my family members live in the United States, but most of them live in Hong Kong, China. Every December, my mom, dad, and I go to Hong Kong to visit family and friends. Hong Kong is over 6,000 miles away from the U.S. My grandparents and great aunts do not speak English, so I speak Cantonese with them.

I began to like origami when I was in kindergarten. I still like folding paper into different shapes and objects because it is challenging and fun. I have had to learn how to read the diagrams and to follow directions carefully. I hope to invent something one day that will benefit the world, just like the origami master, Dr. Robert Lang. I am proud of my origami productions and like to share them.

I completed this book with the support of my mom and dad. I hope my book will help other children see that it is possible to make their dreams come true. I would love to hear about your projects and I am sure I will learn a lot from you as well.

Most Sincerely,

Justin Tsin

覃正贤

About Origami

All the animal figures and paper crafts in this book were handmade by the author using an ancient art called origami.

Origami（折り紙）—literally meaning "folding paper"— is the art of paper folding. The art of origami is to take a piece of paper and fold it in a way that it becomes a new object. Even though it is originally from Asia, the word "origami" usually refers to any type of paper folding art.

Origami only uses a few types of common folds and creases. These can be combined in different ways to produce a variety of results. In general, origami designs begin with a square sheet of paper, whose sides may be different colors, and usually proceed without cutting or fastening the paper.

References

You can find instructions and tips to create the origami figures in this book in the following websites and books:

Bats
http://art-smart.ci.manchester.ct.us/easy-bat/easy-bat.html

Birds
Nakano, Dokuotei. (1997). *Origami Classroom II: Boxed Set.* Tokyo, Japan: Japan Publications Trading.

Chickens
Fukumoto, Jodi. (2005). *The Guide to Hawaiian-Style Origami Charms.* Waipahu, HW: Island Heritage Publishing.

Crabs
Origami Making Kit/Sea Life. 4M Industrial Development Limited. Web site: www.4m-ind.com

Cuboctahedron
Fuse, Tomoko. (1990). *Unit Origami: Multidimensional Transformations.* Tokyo, Japan: Japan Publications.

Dragons
Montroll, John. (1996). *Mythological Creatures and the Chinese Zodiac in Origami.* Mineola, NY. Dover Publications.

Frogs
Johnson, Anne Akers. (2003). *Origami.* Palo Alto, CA: Klutz.

Ladybugs
Van Sicklen, Margaret. (2005). *The Joy of Origami.* New York, NY: Workman Publishing Company, Inc.

Lotus Flowers
LaFosse, Michael G. (2004). *Origami Flowers Folded Kit.* Boston, MA: Tuttle Publishing.

Pagoda Towers
Van Sicklen, Margaret. (2005). *The Joy of Origami.* New York, NY: Workman Publishing Company, Inc.

Parrots
Johnson, Anne Akers. (2003). *Origami.* Palo Alto, CA: Klutz.

Peacocks
Nakano, Dokuotei. (1997). *Origami Classroom II: Boxed Set.* Tokyo, Japan: Japan Publications Trading.

Pinwheels
Kasahara, Kunihiko. (1998). *Origami Omnibus: Paper Folding for Everyone.* Tokyo, Japan: Japan Publications.

Seals
Johnson, Anne Akers. (2003). *Origami.* Palo Alto, CA: Klutz.

Art

1 Observe the artwork in the book. Ask children to describe their favorite pages in the book and give reasons for their choices.
2 Discuss the history of origami or paper folding.
3 Provide opportunities for children to do origami artwork.
4 Provide opportunities for children to write Chinese characters using paintbrushes and draw or show pictures that explain the meaning of the characters.

Literacy Skills

1 Use imagination to compose a piece of creative writing based on a specific artwork.
2 Learn/review/practice conditional sentence structure.
3 Write a letter to the author.

Mathematics

1 Learn/review/practice counting by 3s.
2 Reinforce the multiplication concept and work with multiples of 3.
3 Identify even and odd numbers.
4 Learn/review symmetry. Use actual paper folding to explore the concept.

Chinese Language Skills

1 Learn about classifiers.
  In English, a speaker refers to "two books" (number + noun). Chinese speakers refer to the number + classifier + book, adding the word "ben" to refer to the class of nouns. So in the Chinese language a word is added in between the actual number and the noun.

2 Practice conditional sentence structure and classifiers by making new sentences using the model given by the book. This activity can be combined with the project suggested in the Critical Thinking Skills & Project Ideas section on page 32.

Chinese Culture

1 Discuss the benefits of knowing more than one language and culture.

2 Discuss the Chinese meanings for certain animals and numbers. For example, in China, the dragon is the symbol for emperors. Also, the number nine connotes longevity and is considered the most desirable number.

3 Discuss colors and their symbolism. Red is a lucky color in the Chinese culture and gold is the color for royalty. Red and gold colors are often used for celebrations.

Critical Thinking Skills & Project Ideas

1 Discuss the challenges that the young author might have faced in the process of creating the project shown in this book—the artwork and the creative writing.
2 Discuss the challenges that the young author might have faced in the process of getting this book published.
3 Brainstorm questions that children would like to ask the author of this book.
4 Explain that the author of this book had a talent (paper folding & creative writing), a specific interest (learning Mandarin), and a dream (getting a book published), and he put those three things together in a project that eventually became this book. Invite children to think of their particular talents, interests, and dreams, and to come up with a project they could engage in to accomplish their goals.
5 Ask children to share their own project ideas. Discuss the steps they might take to complete their projects. Encourage them to put their thoughts into actions! Don't forget to support them as needed along the process.

This book truly reflects a labor of love between mother and son. Justin wanted to create an origami book and his mom wanted to sustain his interest in learning Mandarin through engaging in this project. It is an example of a parent guiding her son to help make his dreams come true. Children are never too young to accomplish big goals!

DATE DUE

APR 2 2			
APR 0 4			
GAYLORD			PRINTED IN U.S.A.